THE BETWEEN

LIGHT AND DARK

Poems on the

Stages from Childhood to Adult-
hood

Penny Sage

Copyright © 2024 Penny Sage. All rights reserved.
All rights reserved, including the right to reproduce this book of portions thereof in any form whatsoever. No part of this publication may be reproduced, distributed, or transmitted in any form by any means including photocopying, recording, or other electronic or mechanical methods, without prior permission of the publisher, For permission, contact leila@remedyreads.com

Illustrations by Penny Sage

ISBN: 979-8-88525-681-0 - ebook
ISBN: 979-8-88525-670-4 - paperback

Second edition 2024
Visit: www.remedyreads.com

@remedyreads

DEAR READER

I hope this book guides you and encourages you through any waves that you face, and always remember, you are not alone and nothing lasts.

DISCLAIMER

There are references to violence, depression and other sensitive topics, read at your discretion.

DEDICATION

To my parents who have guided me, loved me and supported me unconditionally. Thank you for making me who I am today.

The Teenagers

Whisked away by the future,
Tormented by the present,
Neglecting the past.

Taking first steps as a person, individual,
Without succumbing—

Sports Life

I hobble at only 17.
My knees crack and pop—
Hey, it's fireworks!
Why, you ask?
It's simple. I blew my knees!
Sports are a pain.
Oh, that's quite literal!
Whiplash killed my neck—
Scoliosis, well, it's just a nuisance.
My hips no longer function.
Knees are double, triple in their size.
My ankles and feet—oh geez, don't bother!
But hey! The sport was interesting.
Gave me plenty of memories,
Doctors, insurance...
Hold up! I'm coming!

Getaway Rides

Oldies tumble out my radio.
Sun pierces my skin through glass.
Wind dancing across faces—
Freeing my hair from the knots on my head.
I surf across highways,
Traffic the only thing between me and flight—

The sun is ahead.
I push forward, escaping my small world,
Riding toward the sun—
My freedom.

Teen Wage

$0.00 in my bank account.
My stomach knots.
Driving is over.
Fun is only possible with others' money.
Shops are merciless—
Slapping sings of "help wanted,"
Only to say "18 and older."

Limited by age as we are young,
Limited by experience as we grow old.
Limits bordering our lives.
Jobs take months to get,
And seconds to lose.

Then everyone asks—
Why are teens always broke?
Well, here's your answer:
Getting a job is no joke.

Honest Truths

Do I like him?
That's of no importance.
In reality, you will never get a true answer.
Not when wearing skins of honesty
Means to bring certain death, as to
soldiers with no armory.

Honesty is redundant commentary
When everyone lies.
Save themselves, save another—
What's the harm?
I'm not the one breaking your arm.

False Life

Why so stressed?
I work in a battlefield
Where hormones are mines,
And everyone knows that soon,
Life, as we know it, will cease to exist.
Yeah, it's "only" high school.
But it's also a life, a job,
Where bills must be paid daily,
Where multiple bosses with varying moods steal your free time,
And where coworkers—don't bother!
They can be worse!

High school is a job, a lifestyle.
You clock out at 3, but don't end your days until 1.
Mounds of work are to be done.
Forget a life—
You signed it away to your "real job."
Tests are payday,
GPAs are promotions.
Be friendly—but not too friendly.
Everything is a competition.
Don't do extra? Ha!
You're either a flake or lazy.
Something is not right if you don't have anxiety.
You aren't giving enough of your life if you are not depressed.

Stress? If only it was only that.
You're left, still wondering how to live life.
But don't worry! It'll all be over soon!
College is coming—
Where it all starts again—only this time,
They'll take your money, too!

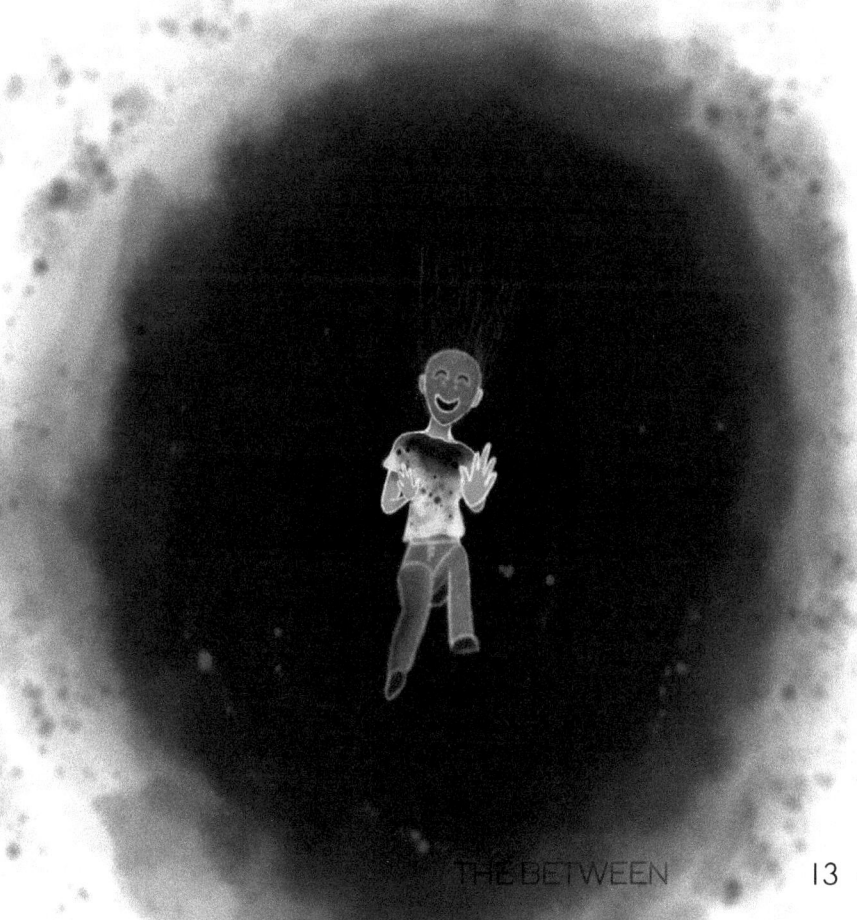

PENNY SAGE

Summer

Summer comes after blooming
flowers in the spring,
Before the leaves shrivel and die.
It's the fleeting expansion of passion.

What is love? It is summer.

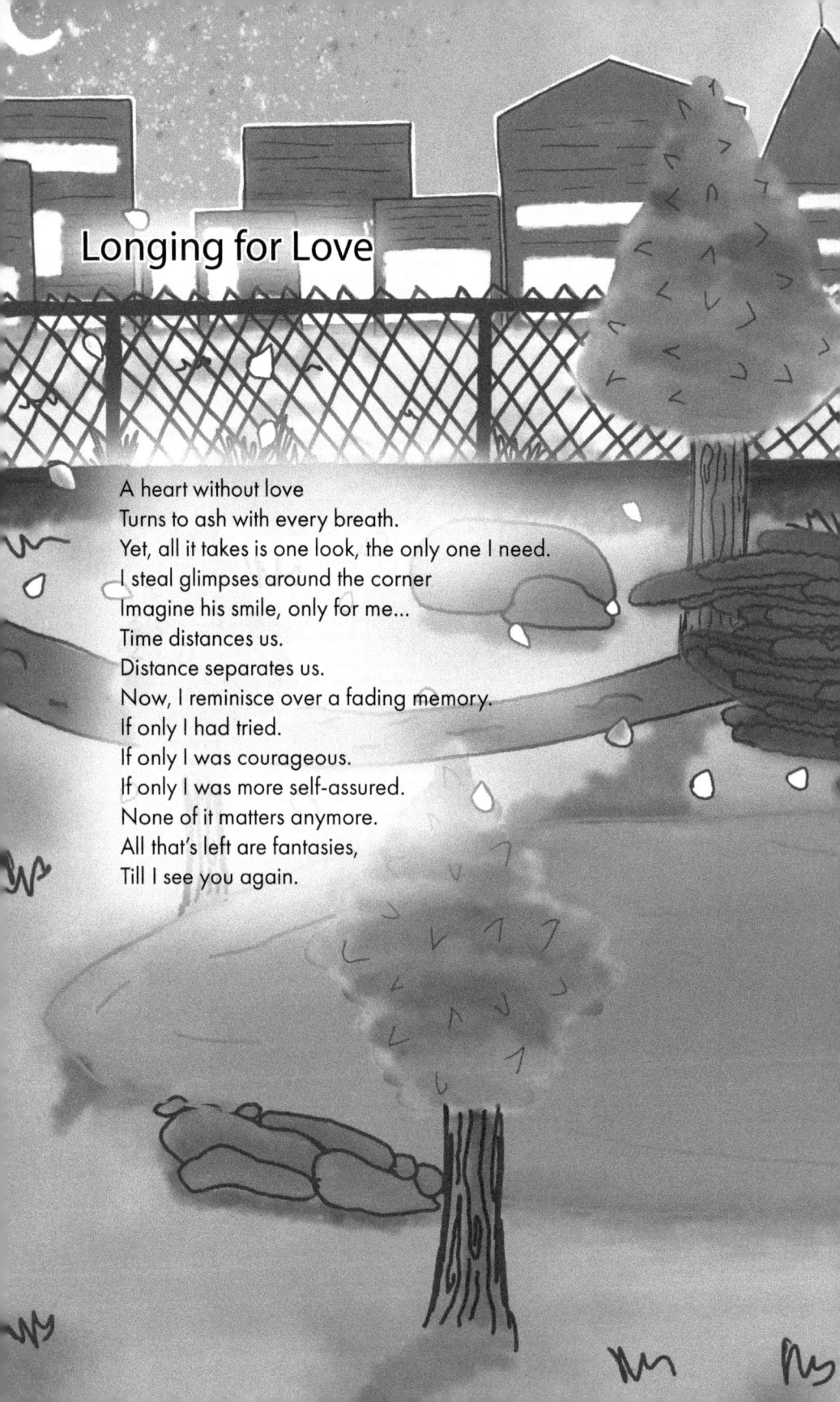

Longing for Love

A heart without love
Turns to ash with every breath.
Yet, all it takes is one look, the only one I need.
I steal glimpses around the corner
Imagine his smile, only for me...
Time distances us.
Distance separates us.
Now, I reminisce over a fading memory.
If only I had tried.
If only I was courageous.
If only I was more self-assured.
None of it matters anymore.
All that's left are fantasies,
Till I see you again.

Marathon

Legs thumping
Adrenaline racing
Feet throbbing—
Thu-thunk, thu-thunk.

Lungs collapsing
Veins pulsating

Hands clammy with sweat
Reaching the core of blistering sores
A marathon.

How long can the body last
Along a never ending path?

Organs dropping into your soles
Reaching the core of blistering sores
Mind racing in panicked focus

Beckoning a past of disdain.
Cluttered, tormented with turbulence
A mind compromised by history.

Bodies blur,
Sprinting past cheers and markers
Shoes becoming faded shreds of rubber—

The runners persist,
Living each moment
Breath—for breath—

Reaching the sunrise,
Carrying themselves high
Traveling on autopilot,
Willing their bodies to make it.
Hearts only travel so far.

Fighting past the misery,
Heart beating for every revelry
Each moment pushing a runner father
Without mind or body,
Beyond limits,
Striving toward endless possibilities—

Until the finish line is crossed,
Where the runner greets their defeated challenger:
A beaten road, worn and weary,
Full of high lows. They are facing the cheering—

Respectful nod,
Calm peace of the gentle breeze,
Leaving the runner, and the path
Fulfilled.

THE BETWEEN

Vengeance of a Heart

Hearts are burdens we all carry,
Guarded, within the fortress impenetrable.
But my heart, it sags.
As it bleeds out
It burns,

Clouded within a haze of pain.
I can't understand, and
No longer do I wish to.
I hope this is what you wanted.

You broke my heart.
Now, consumed by this pain,
I bestow you the gift of misery.

Both of us fall,
Downwards, into a spiral.
Deeper the hollowness settles;
Darker our love taints

Until all we touch becomes a victim
Of the pain we never shake.

Looking Unto Heavens

By daylight, soft warmth cuddles me;
By nightfall, stars spark roaring fires within.

Each day, bricks pile on my shoulders—
Shoulders you would soothe.
Each day with you was always a mystery—
If only they were longer.

Lately, it's been hard to get by.
No life is worth living
Without my best friend beside me.
Dear Lord, treat him well.
Tell him that I'll love him always.
Dear Lord, keep him safe.
I'll never forget him.

By daylight, soft warmth cuddles me;
By nightfall, stars spark roaring fires within.

Looking out at cotton clouds and the bright yellow sun,
All I can ever think of is you.
Your voice soothed my ears,
Keeping my heart in rhythm.
Your love filled me,
And I never felt loneliness.
You stole my heart, once,
And I can't wait for you to steal it again—
In the afterlife.

Weeping Willows

You must not forget,
Not when the sun sets, nor water becomes desecrated,
That your darling, weeping, willow, sleeps near the bay.
Her leaves shudder,
Tumbling to the ground.
Her massive trunk sways with the wind.
Don't forget her, please.

She longs for your hand to stroke her trunk—
She longs for the days you sat upon her roots—
She longs for your love once more—
She longs for you.

Dear willow,
Sorrowful beauty,
Stuck in times of love and light,
Broken by her love—
Her tears shall flood the bay,
Wiping away everything she touches.

No longer are critters swinging on her dangling branches.
No longer do animals lay underneath, comforting her.
No longer are you there.

The weather has become harsher.
Now naked,
Standing in the bitter cold,
She rattles with every snowflake—
Yet she stands.
Waiting for you.
Every day, she holds onto memories of you.
You never loved her,
Did you?

Finding You

Hard and diligently I have worked,
To feel worthy of a simple smile.
For the mere thought of your graces, I would give
My sun—
My moon—
My falling stars—only to you.
But I know my heart will only ache
To be given the honors of loving.
For I am plentiful in demons,
And I am plain in face...

Love me anyway.
I am no more perfect than a rat. Please forgive me.
I've been longing
For a friend,
A partner
With whom to share an eternity.
When you're willing,
I will open my soul.
Until then, forever I shall wait.

PENNY SAGE

A Voice's Cry

Bullets murder the
body. Knives sever through flesh.
Only words stain souls.

Its Voice in Me

Chilled wind crawls across the fjord,
Along my spine.
The whistles ring within symphonies
Along the river—
Can you hear it?
It's the voice of the valley.
Delicate and powerful,
It's the hand of the elder tree.
It's the fire in animal underbellies.

A voice that is as natural as a breath of air,
The delicacy of a flower, the speed of a hare.
Thunderous and instantaneous, lightning,
A boar that hollers, an insect chirping, shrieking.
In the sea I swim, drowning in the muffled
expanse of noise—

In the city I lurk, crawling like a zombie,
muted sound aloft.
Here, I must make sense of jumbled,
frantic banters.
Here, I must make my own voice.

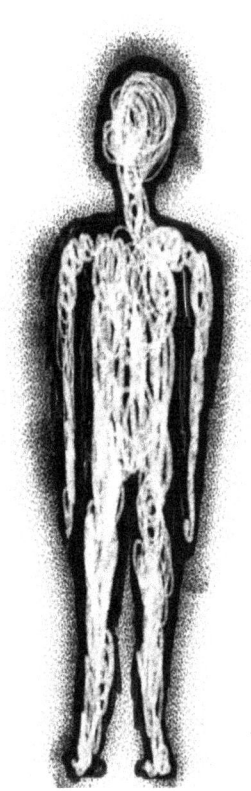

A Page

There are many words to be said on a blank page.

Configured

For what?

For showing something has been felt.

Words are to be experienced.

Everyone is the center of their story,

But there is always more than one who takes

importance.

Inside the pages of a book,

The stanzas of a poem,

Real people exist.

What's been written seems so real,

You feel it too—

And maybe you aren't alone, anymore.

One's Own

There lies a thin sheet—
Glossy white, a mirror.
Time and time again,
A sheet bursts with life.

Far into creations, an artist wanders,
Going farther than the sky, to the sun's waking horizon.
A possession no longer—

Art is given life, painted, carved,
Never leaving mindless eyes.
Viper eyes hiss and snare—

What's created never belonged
In a place of monochrome and sameness,
Left lost and forgotten, tumbling into the ocean's trash bag.

Language

Words
Are faster than any bullet;
Stronger than an atomic bomb.
Words, phrases, sentences,
Channeling emotions through
To connect.
From our first hello, to our final goodbye,
As air passes, one last time.
Something so simple—
Connected to everything we touch.
Healing grace,
Our tool of love, faith, happiness.
Deathly virus.
Our weapon of fear, hate, division.
Use it for power—
Use it for action—
Language keeps us connected.
Words, beliefs, cultures,
Differences only build you higher.
Many definitions, many more meanings—
Words.

Rotting Beauty

The old man is alive within his art,
Creating miracles with a single thought.
The feeling of warmth from art's moving beauty—
We have experienced something greater,
But it takes its toll, doesn't it?
Why must a man who gives so much
Possess so many demons?
You see evils—
Conquering them with your art.
Another day, another possibility,
Another struggle.
You're not alone,
Please don't go—
Someone, show him his magic,
Before another Van Gogh is lost.

Dance, Ballerina

In my dreams, dancers glide across the floor
Sweeping up shimmering dust in twilight.
They soar as angels loving music, like no one else.
A stage is their home,
Living, breathing for dance —
Their hearts beat to the rhythm of music.
It mustn't be taken away.

Dancers aren't humans.
They are the soul, will, and emotion of music.
Grand jeté, pirouette —
They become alive onstage.
Smiles so genuine —
Please, don't take them away.

It's dark onstage, quiet in anticipation.
Don't take them.
Until bright lights are lit from above —

And I wake from my dreams.
And there is no other place for a ballerina to be.

Spoken in Disdain

The person who has words seldom expresses them—
The person who defends moral equities is the first to break liberties—
The person who is angry at the world is cussing at dust,
Yet a grin staples them together, screaming peace, love, and happiness.

The mind, which is jumbled,
Ignorant of left side to right side
Makes everything blur. Reality morphs to insanity.
Air feels heavy, double-speaking double-negatives—
Rethink, rethink, of yet another possibility,
Then—nothing.

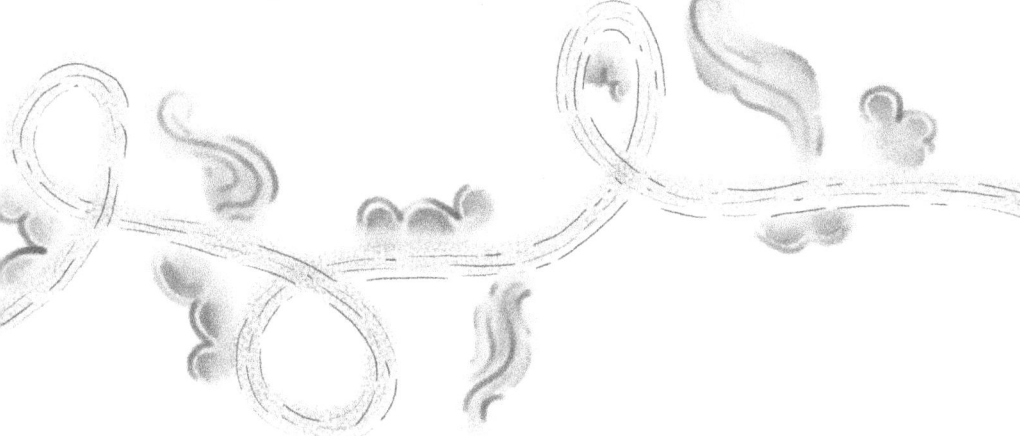

Everything is blank, the words spewed out are fake—
And you glitch, frozen.
What you say is logical, yet feels so improbable.
Split into two, and there's nothing you can do.
Confined by the bars of your cage,
Your body can't be dismayed.
The turmoil will just have to fade.
The words in the mind are altered all the time—
Faces contorting to revulsion
At the sound of words
Never meant to be heard.

THE BETWEEN

Stained words

From the backs of fiery mouths,
Words of passion are sent out—
But for you,
To ash they settle.
Justice has not served you,
Man with Cries of Silence.
Let them watch as you rot
Withering.
It would have been easy to stop this, to fix you,
Old Man, who lives in silence,
supported by a cane and more silence.
If only you were to say something.
Fall to your silence, while I scramble toward the light,
You coward.

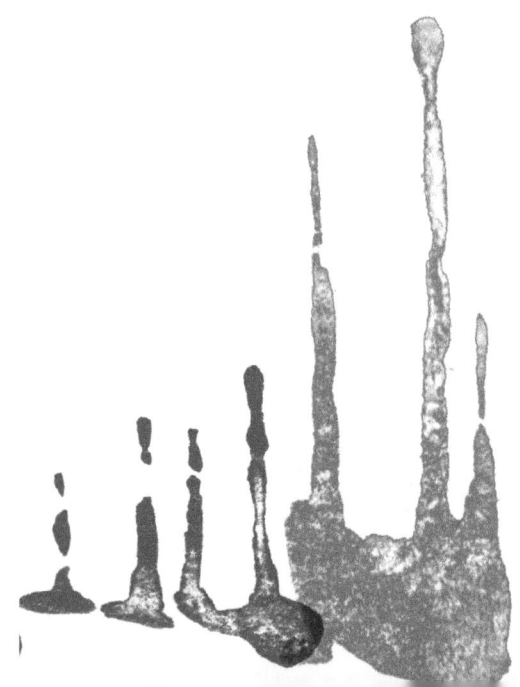

Forever Unfinished

It's a poem.
A series of articulated, calculated words
Expressing emotions, feelings, otherwise avoided.
Instead of confronting,
I leave the contents of my heart exposed.

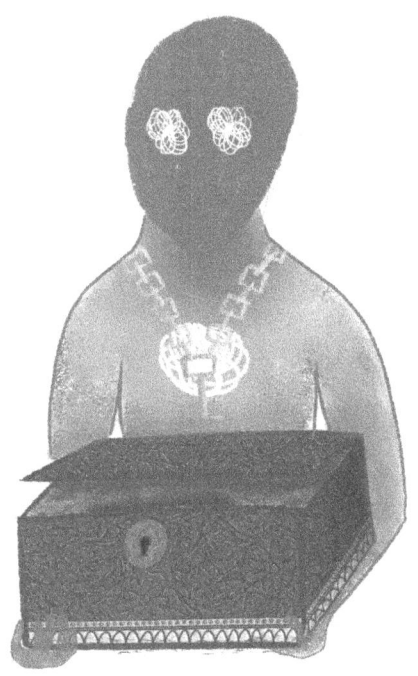

Fall

Time passes with each drifting leaf.
The season of all seasons.
Time is at its slowest
When the ground is unearthed
With the simple and complicated clash.
Fall is turbulent chaos—

Wishful Façade

Dancing across paths of shooting stars and fireflies,
Light as air, twirling within resplendent dresses, twinkling eyes,
No longer confined, Earth's gravity lifts them high—
Weights fall, skipping meteors plummet down, *rebirth*.
Echoes ricochet, beating music into a deformed Earth.
Vanquished are plaguing nightmares, absolved are all fears.

Shimmering lights, guiding stars,
Speed of light, traveling far.
Solitary peace, desire,
Far from reach, grasping to hold.

Only magic floats about, making any dream possible.
A life of splendor, nothing is untouchable.
Heads full of light, without thought—every star morphs reality.

Steal your miracles, reaching further than your touch,
Kissing each star tenderly, the entrapment of heaven's jewels.
Destiny is altered, pirated treasure fades.
The impossible, never supposed to be—stars are wishes,
Rescinded dreams.
Reality no longer.

Passage of Time

I know nothing of the time that ticked by
Before I arrived—
Yet here I am,
With a heart of petroleum,
Day by day,
As if everything were the same.

Tick-tock, tick-tock,
Yet again, time passes me.
Every day that sunrise peaks,
Looming light over my closed eyes.

Things will be done, deadlines have been met.
Though, that tick-tock time,
Still hushes secrets into my ear,

Hopelessly charming me with dreams of another life.
A place where time was mine.
Duties vanish, restraints cease
In those dreams, and I am as light as air.

Tick-tock, tick-tock,
And sadly,
Time passes me by.
And I do not listen.

Continuing Credits

Curtains polish a stage,
levered into the frame,
Showcasing masks that
were never real.

Within the skin of another's life,
Witnessing another reality,
an onlooker veiled in a void.
Never seen, never heard,
Eyes open wide,
Critical of every mistake.

Curtains, a performer's veil
Hiding imperfections, each quiver,
Every stutter—
Nothing is ever truly hidden.

Eyes open wide,
Curtains drape over windows, giving
Glimpses into our lives,
Stolen within commodity homes.

It's one thing to be connected—
Another to be stalked.
When all is blackened,
The curtains lower, and prying strangers
Await a new performance.

THE BETWEEN

Average Days

Wake up to a world colored in gray,
Stanzas copied and pasted,
Time, looped of routine days.

Endless moments
Trapped in a locked box,
Buried within a closet,
Covered in dust.

Treating a most valuable savior
As a thing that doesn't matter.

Sunrise is just a sunrise,
Rain can only be rain,
And yet, it has the power
To sustain, or impede.

No matter when you wake,
Days will never cease.

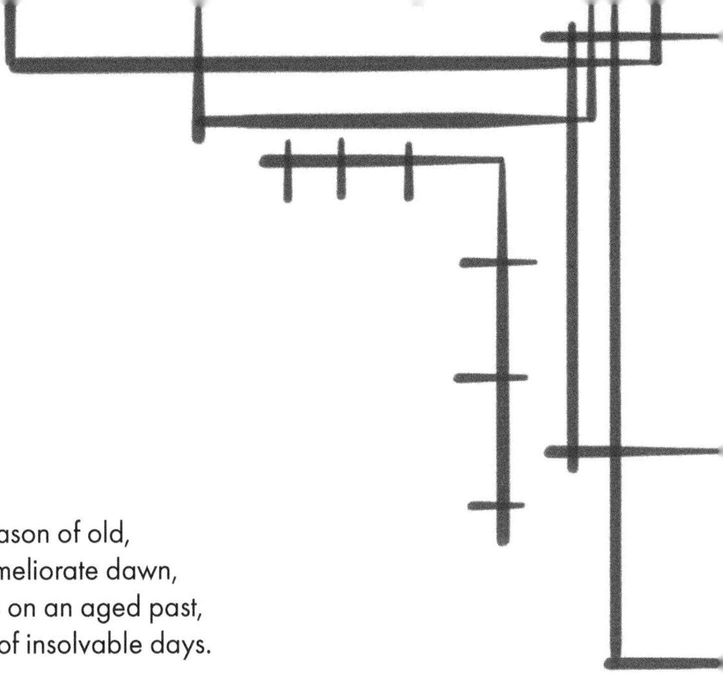

Mundane is a season of old,
Fabricating an ameliorate dawn,
Casting shadows on an aged past,
On the dreariest of insolvable days.

And yet, a person continues
Living for happy moments,
Riding tides on the backs of whales,

And a person persists,
Walking blindly, carrying
The past into the future.

Pushing forth with determination
And curiosity about what's next,
Overcoming dread for what's ahead,
A person must carry on—as

A writer must write.

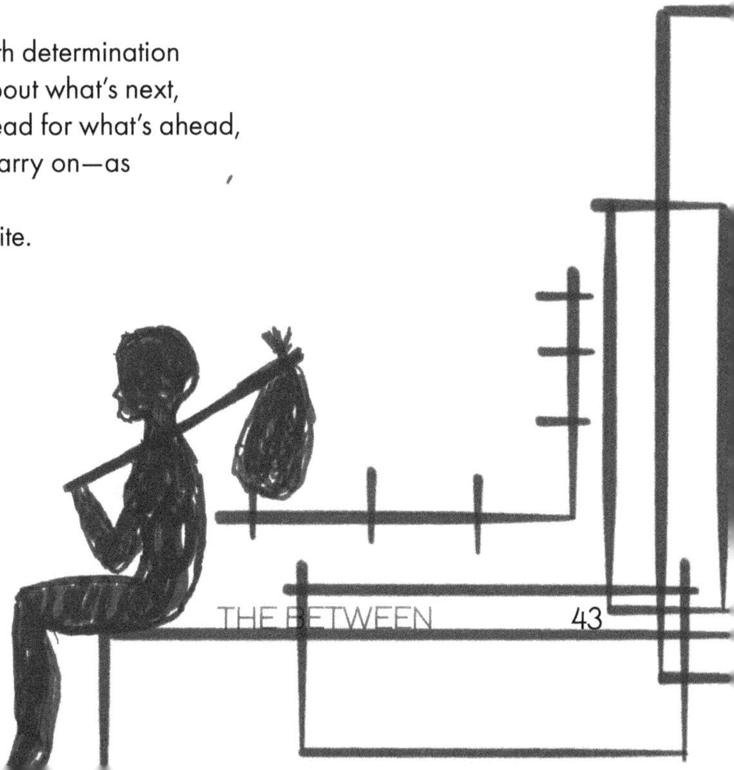

Laughing Sun

The sun rises,
Parting the deep sea,
Crawling, inch by inch,
To the tops of the sky—
The sun laughs.

It laughs, ablaze with light,
Radiating heat,
Roaring spitfire, it laughs.
The sun, darn that sun.

Far from all
Yet, any closer,
All would be cinders.
Evil sun from hell,
A great deity, my god, oh sun!
Heaven and hell bestow trickery upon me.

The sun which laughs
Is the very sun that leaves
When the dead of night comes
To rain hellish nightmares upon me.

Warm kisses sprinkled across my skin no more.
Lights peering down,
Compensating for a sun no longer there.
It's when all is no more that you leave,

Out to play, mingling through conversations,
Participating well beyond the end of day...
But when the eyes leave, the cold lingers.
My sun turns astray.
Yet, you will not leave forever, I say.

And you laugh.

Fading Senses

The whiff of a scent
Strokes the hairs within my nose—how familiar.
It feels so warm. It's where I was. Now, where I went.

What to make of the whispers a past that never leaves,
Constricting my lungs, fighting to breathe?
In an instant, it's faded—
Now only my reminiscence.

Before Crickets

Before the crickets sing
Mornings are dark. Empty—
All has fallen softly asleep,
Everyone's voice silenced.
A moon and its stars dangle like dancing mobiles,
Lulling the sleepless to their dreams,
Calming someone's turbulent present,
Awakening another's mind as they witness the beyond.

Emerging from drunken mists of dreams,
Few wake up to see a waning moon's goodbye,
Watching for a new day to arise,
God silent by their side.

Enchantments

Smooth rockies,
Fashionable shoes tentative,
Beats thumping, reverberating
through floorboards.
Dance to the heart of jazz
And within trance, all fall.

Lively, melancholy,
Tentative, rambunctious,
It's the world of music—
The herders of sheep.

Entranced by the sounds,
Entrapped within the
corners and cracks
Of this bizarre world.

Within those hypnotic notes
Minds swirl,
Entering bizarre worlds

Alice in Wonderland.

Cigars, and cigarettes,
That haze of mystified calm,
Persuading everyone to play along.

Melody's voice has come,
In unison, mouths mumble
Harmonious words
Echoed with no thought.

Smooth is the drum,
The soul of tempo
Lollygagging everyone along.

Until that crack of dawn
We all play make believe
with the tempo
Of a smooth jazz song.

Repetative Pleasantries

Melted cheese dangles from the air.
Left ingrained, a fragrance of zest—
Just at the tip of your tongue.

Something of a warmth holds you captive.
Already, your mouth is infused with saliva—
Strings of cheese melted and seasoned to the highest perfection.

Baked goods are so sweet, it's overpowering,
Intoxicating.
Meandering thoughts simply vanish
As that bite is hungrily, slowly, savored—

Then it's all gone, the monster is satiated.
Grumbling, it lay tossing and turning
And slowly you feel like a big swollen thumb.

But once a smell is tasted,
Just at the tip of your tongue...
You take a bite, to savor every flavor,
And like a bursting soda can,
Everything is over.

Not too long,
You're right back where you started.

Lost to the Wind

Four corners—winds blow
Traveling dim sunrises,
Fall's season fading.

Us, and I

Which am I?
A mirror, or the mirage of whomever
stands near me?
Do I fade and disappear with each relationship?
Do I become them?
Or am I still me?

Conclusions

You prefer your own conclusions
Over asking hard questions.
Not everything is as it seems.
Not everyone is black or white.

The aroma of fresh coffee is comforting.
Sitting in isolation—refreshing.
I don't need you here, so don't talk to me.

Ignore me, as you used to do.
For after all this time, you still don't know me.
You never tried to know me, did you?

Give

Within the tunnel of thought, where all is dark and damp,
A single light shimmers, dancing
Within the tunnel, under panicked cars and creaking buses.
The walls shift, swaying each way.

Without beginning or end,
A shrinking black hole it creates.
Yet, that fairy light persists,
A twinkle that resists.

The panicked fear sparks a firestorm,
Igniting the body to fight—
Legs pumping wildly, desperation comes forth
as greedy with starvation,
I snatch the light.

So gently I cradle it,
lovingly as a baby.
Soothing tears with
gentle lullabies
And settled quaking walls.
Diminished, Apnea's fingers
unravel.

Fairy light, the greatest
treasure,
Newfound demise.
Things are tricky—
A tool, a crutch, then all
consuming.

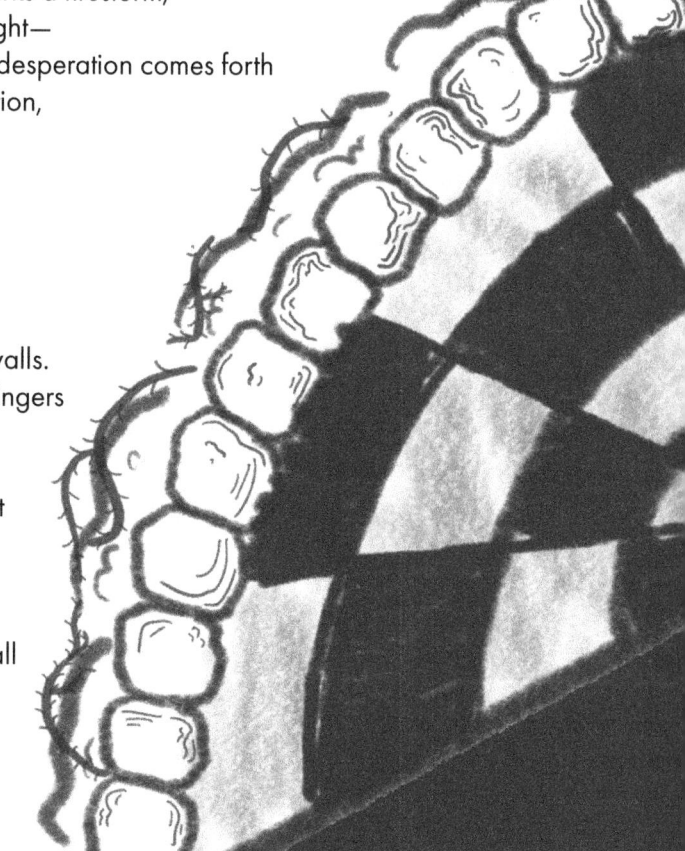

An infatuation for a thing,
And a person is pulled underground.
The fairies continuously rise to the top,
Protected within my hands grip,
Keeping me afloat.

It's that feeling we all search for,
We all reach toward—
The rise in dopamine,
an ease of calmness
Settling the fiercest seas
What we don't have, what we
aren't given, we take.

Each one of us are human—
Human, and vulnerable.
Longing chokes,
desperation drowns,
envy destroys.

That fairy light seeps into
skin,
Burrowing deep,
Hiding inside,

Until I am it,
and it is me,
And no longer
do any burdens
eat me away.

THE BETWEEN

Humans Can't Talk

> It's been a long time
> Since I have seen you walking by.
> Day by day we talk—
> Yet, what does it mean to talk, at a distance?
> Sending pics with words?
> Small clips and minimal phrases?
> Texts covered in emojis?

> Everything but simple conversations—
> Small moments of time
> When people gathered
> Face-to-face, merely to say, "hi."
> The art of communication
> Dwindles with each
> passing generation.
> Consolidated by false truths—
> Lies to ourselves and others.
> What is a real relationship?

If there ever was such a thing, it was
Replaced, so easily,
With screens and things
in need of attention.
Minimally
We are driven by our
own desires and needs,
Our own selfishness and narcissism.

Communication becomes
a one-way road:
Talk when needed,
Respond when necessary.
Words may spew out the mouth
Speaking the tongues of Christ
Or Shakespeare's sonnets
of binding love—
But will it be heard?
Will there be a response?
Or will you stroke your
finger to the left
With unknown silence,
leaving a voice unheard
From far, far, away?

Ugly Face

A hand grazes cool glass
Framing a face
Looking nothing like me.

Fractals continuing infinitely—
This isn't me,
Deep whispers echo loudly.

A mirror,
Showing me my hate, misery,
And vanity—I wish they were fake.

Do I conceal it, or accept it?
Beautiful
Ugly Face.

Evolved Souls

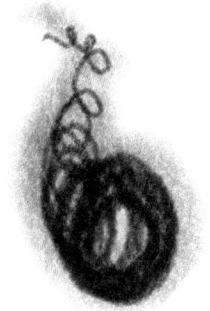
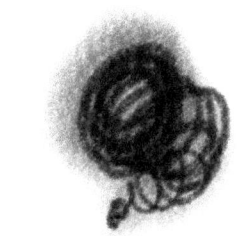

Hot and cold
Siblings, sisters, family—
Separated.
Couldn't stand each other
Yet, never wanted to leave.
As seasons, we changed.
No longer playing at petty fights,
We talk.
We laugh, we hug, we cry
Despite the distance.

We never were the same, you and I,
Nor have we always seen eye to eye.
But we've gotten older,
And now, I would never wander.

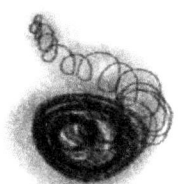
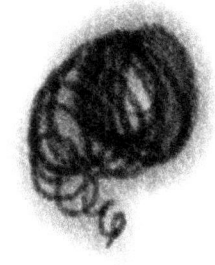

Weight Has Been Lifted

It's hard not to feel detached.
But you are a stranger, a two-faced fraud.
Your true face can't hide from me any longer.
Such a fool I was—
I should have let you go sooner,
I should have seen through your façade—
No matter.
Your shackles on my limbs are broken, now.

A weight has been lifted—
I'm letting you go.
I walk away
Never happier.
No one saved me
No one rescued me—
I found myself locked in a cage,
And I set her free.

Do what you want, I could not care less.
I found what I wanted.
Your words won't hurt me,
Your screams don't shatter me.
I am loved.

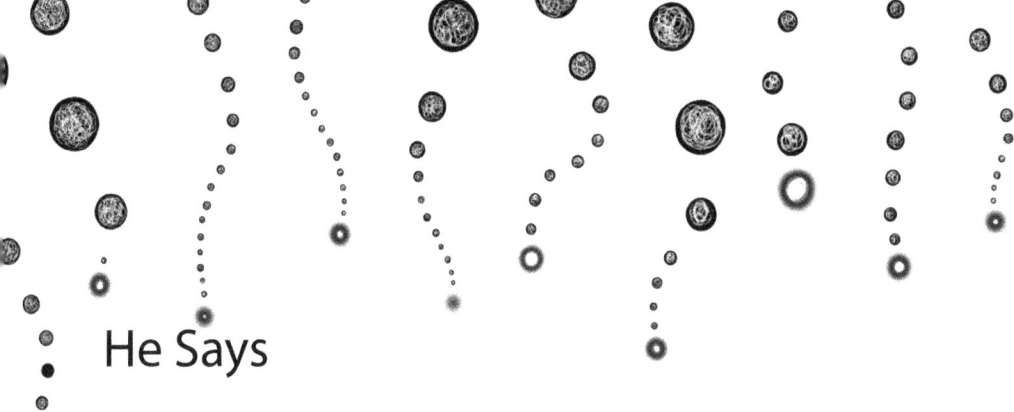

He Says

Mindless clouds
Drift through air—
Space and time tear.
Nothing is amiss
In the grand expanse
Of nothing.

Is it even possible?
He says.
To be lost and found?

To know everything
Yet, still be an apprentice—
Is to be dust.
All-inhabiting, everywhere—
And still minuscule,
In the entirety of the universe.

Aware of the world,
Without knowing yourself...

Mindless clouds
Traveling far and wide.

Lift me high,
He says.
Teach me,
He begs.

Clouds of luster
Glittering under moonlight—
Pause.
Become me, and
I shall become you.
Ever-growing
Constantly learning
The endless evolution of life.

Petals

A dandelion seed trickles downward
along the narrow road,
Traveling by water,
animal, and wind,
Seeing things that it will not forget,
Hearing things it'd wish
to only be dreams.

The dandelion suddenly realizes
it's no longer seen as a seed.
As its roots grow, it becomes taller.
The flower buds, from the ugly
duck to a swan, transform.
It has become much older now,
and, being the beaut that it is,
Is flaunting and daunting
others, showing its confidence,
power, and ravishing petals
Before its final days, slowly decaying
inside.

The dandelion had
considered itself a flower

With delicate, plump petals
that shimmer in rain
And long, slender stalks
that keep itself upright.
Yet others only see
A weed
Meant for extermination.
All they count are ugly scars
that seem so evident—like
the color of your skin.

Petals fall off its body
Making it, oh-so-naked and afraid.
Its green stalk is now
brown and scarred.

People have killed dandelions,
Leaving nothing but betrayal
and hurt from the footprints
of their departure.
With bated breath the dandelion
releases its final seeds
Before resting in the dirt
from which it came.

Find Me

Can I be found?
Staring out toward acres of fields, I know that
Once, there was identity,
Long before. A purpose.

Aimlessly wandering within fjords of the wild, I know that
Anything can be found.

From green stalks,
Thousands of colored petals flutter like fireflies
Coloring cotton clouds, weaving like wind through heavens.
And again I ponder—
Who, what, am I?
With a sense of purpose, am I lost?
And can I be found?

PENNY SAGE

Winter

Don't cry for every ache, or you will freeze under silent snowflakes.
Everything is marked by foreboding, cold, and hungry snow, consuming any and all things.
Look up—there's nothing there.
Look down, and be met with the absence of what was not there before.
Snowflakes make puddles of tears as they melt on your cheeks.
This is the darkest season.

The Fallen

A raindrop ripples onto the surface of the water,
Sinking like iron,
Setting atop something forgotten,
Something organic in its composition—
Unrecognizable,
This thing is consumed
Into a big puddle of abyss, murkiness,
And the forgotten.

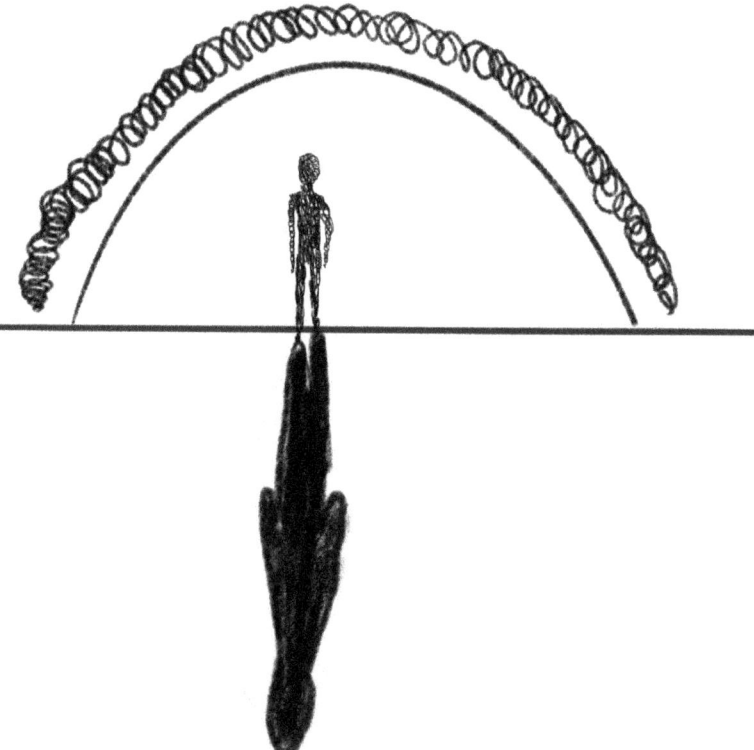

Grave Diggers

People withering away
Tipping over like tombstones.
Stay away—
Stay in the fog—
Stay with the masses.
Big Brother will save you.
Big Brother, ironclad armor, sole eyes only
visible to law and truth.
Big Brother is always watching.
The division from a people to persons,
Forcing a reality that can no longer be accepted—
No longer ignored.

Maiden of Night

Maiden of night,
Catch me in your dreams.
Let your darkness put me asleep
And traveling beyond consciousness.
I'm ruled by laws on this plain,
So carry me far from my bed
To share dreams with you.

Maiden of night,
Lay me to rest.
The sun has whispered its goodbye.
When that fateful sun sleeps
Behind the lakes, the mountains, and the forest,
So shall I.

Maiden of night,
Sleep is impending.
My eyes grow weary with every breath.
Don't cry, angel—
You aren't alone on this night.

Maiden of night,
Take me away into your dreams
Where dancing is never ending;
Laughter ceases to extinguish;
Smiling faces make my heart melt.
Take me to my freedom, sleeping maiden—
Let me enjoy the wondrous darkness—

Maiden of night.

Plagued by Fear

Taking form of shadows
Looming upon walls—
Your darkest side.
The entity of blooming regret
Plaguing thoughts like deep secrets.
Fear covers the thickest blankets,
Boiling until insanity arrives.
One minute it's two feet away—
Within seconds right behind you.

This is the plague of
The damned—
The restless—
The broken—
Fear conquers far beyond death,
Cradling the weakest of hearts,
Swallowing you whole.

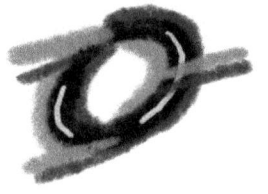

Broken Vinyls

A broken vinyl sputters, in shambles.
70 seconds reappearing in a loop—The loop of life.
You see your past in everything;
It's the only version of ordinary you can recognize.
A repeat, a ruin.
That is why you are afraid of the future.
Because to believe in it
Means to put away the past.

We don't fix vinyl.
They lay forgotten in sleeves of dust,
Or scattered at a dump.

A Settling Darkness

If there is no end to the torment
of an already shriveling
heart;

Let me lie in the fjord.
Digging my feet in wet sand,
I wait for tides to consume me.

White foam hugs my ankles,
fizzes with every teardrop.

I'm saying goodbye,
fading as the sun sets.
Entrapped by memories,
sealed by the past.

Terror consumes every breath,
Your tenacious persona
continuously idle—
Lingering in the back of my mind.
Goodbye.

Racing darkness eats me away in
Seconds, and I struggle to see
above the murky water.

You torment me, my
lingering nightmare,
Never seeming to fade.

Before I sink into the
nothingness of water—

Know that you die with me.
The tickle, the shrill of your
breath creeping behind me—

You, and I, we drift aimlessly
toward gnarly rock.
Ending life as I know it—
Drowning you with it.

A Caged Bird

The bird's wings spread wide with intent to soar,
Gliding among the planes and soft cotton clouds.
Such melodic songs,
A bird has so many things to do.

Nevertheless, Timmy must have a pet,
So a bird he shall get.

Secluded to the dismal inns of a child's
bedroom,
This bird shall never be a bird.
No—it shall only ever become a bird when
its feathers
have gone through the wind—
Eyes glossed, glinting towards the sun.

Little caged bird, confined
to what you've been
given—
Birdie, what do you long for?
Birdie, why must you stay?

Is it really so beautiful,
denying the cage itself?
Illusions may be better than
truths.
Maybe that's why I sense
the bitterness on your beak.

Ominous Journeys

Childhood recollections blur in the back of my mind,
Watching trees float past me, beyond the backseat window.
Gray mists of water and dust settle upon the land, a snow globe—
Monochromatic tones churn roads to
slush.
Slowly, a bleak, forgotten building fades within the mists,
Disappearing, as if never really there.
Swallowed whole
With no resistance.
Mists tug and envelop it ever so snugly,
Before leading the aged building into the mists' abyss.
Forests grow thick and dark, ominous of the past and future.
Trees lump and mold together,
Long, barren trees rooted next to the road, close to tumbling downward—

Look back, only to see broken branches trashing the street
And a dark skyline
Distinguishing skies from the ground.
Soon, we, too, disappear into the misty fog,
The car rolling into the deep.
Eventually everything becomes unseen.

Frozen Moment

One picture
And a moment is captured forever.
Hearty smiles, grinding teeth,
Beautiful clothes draped over fair skin.
A day captured in a lifetime—
A moment prepared for with time and energy,
Only to fade as all memories do with age.
Until time has no meaning,
And people bear no existence.

Impure Light

The brightest smile,
A shining, exploding sun.
Never-ending expansion of energy,
Going, going, traveling toward the darkness.
Comfort, sacred place, home of light—
Take me with you, as you draw moths to your immortal flames.

Yet, they aren't—are they?

As quick as light comes, it simmers and decays.
Left is an aching heart of longing and emptiness.

It was a trap—wasn't it?

Showing brightly, blindingly,
To lure me out of my dark places.
Around and within, before swallowing me whole.
False god, false love, false purity.
Now I pay the price,
Just as a moth—

Dead, and ever falling.

Emotion-less

I walk.
Faces blur into scenery.
All walks of life.
I just pass them by.
I stare at what's ahead—
Nothing in focus—
Noise blaring out of
babies' mouths—

I walk.
I stare at the ground.
Where has it taken me?
Far from where I've been.
I pass my broken relationships,
and remember:

I once knew how to run
As runners do, to be number one.
How cheetahs graze
grass for its prey.

I only walk now.
I realize how little I've done.
Others like me are walking too,
going slow, slowly, slower,
Carrying a mountain of
coal wherever we go.
I see a little girl wailing.
I walk along.

I speak.
Fellow travelers weep.
When did my words mold
into silver bullets,
Shattering someone's core being?
I can no longer lift my head.
Down people fall—SPLAT!
Cantaloupes and watermelons
tumble off shoulders.
I don't have a heart anymore.
When did I lose it?

Departed Doves

What hope a bird must have
When the seasons charge asunder,
Turning bitter, foul, and cold.
Cast away they are,
Shunned from their home.
Freed from all they know.
What hope, when an enraged earth changes before the sun.

But Mother Earth now lies dormant,
Festering in the quake of man.
Oh lord have mercy!
Blessed is the sinful soul
Who inhales pints
Of tears from heaven.
Men of kings and queens are
Mocking the very god bestowing
Land, mountain, and sea.

Many moons have passed
Since the disappearance of departed doves
Forever fleeting in flight.

Dreamless Reality

I don't dream
Only surrender to comforting darkness.
God, don't wake me up.
Let the whole world forget me—
Erase my existence.
I'm not living, I'm not alive.
A corpse mustn't touch the light—
It's sure to bring the blessings of curses
To all it touches.
There is no reason for me here.
People have taken everything from me—
Used me, squeezed out anything I could offer,
Leaving an empty bottle
Trashed among mountains of garbage.
Forgotten.

Family Curses

A man is crying,
Buried within his tormented heart,
Yelling out, anguished by the unfairness of it all.

A woman is drowning
In a bubbly blur of despair,
Laughing at burdens and misery.

A man cowers,
Running toward darkness,
Lying to himself and others about what he truly is.

A woman is fading—
Fighting to stay in a corpse,
Whispering her pain and false promises.

A child is lost.
Invisibly suffering from another's consequences.
The lost child becomes an adult,
Continuing on their family curses.

Tears dampen my shirt
And the cycle continues.

Season's End

Blizzard dies. Sunlight
Streams in, casting snow aside
Winter whispers bye.

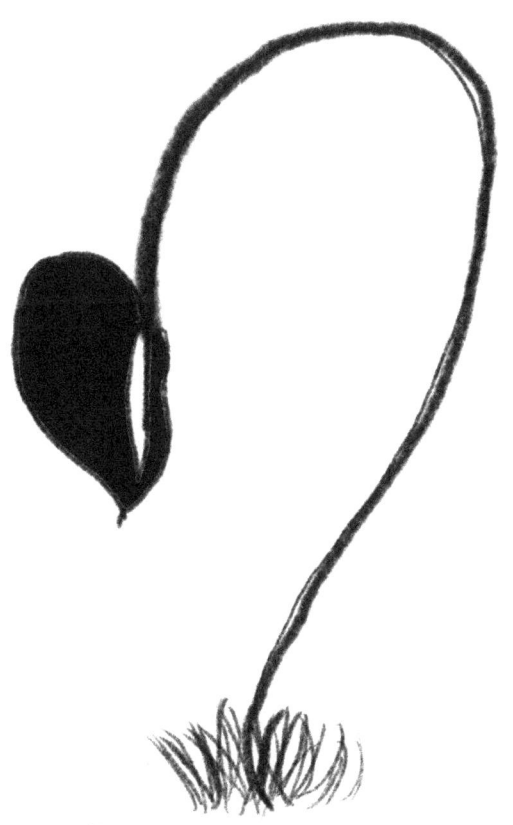

Earth's Tides

Rage, hate, and sorrow give birth to a profound
type of beauty.
It's a rebirth of the human experience.
Closing old chapters, seeking horizons
for the bright sun of tomorrow.

Death's Chime

Blood moon
Draining light from another's life.
The grandfather clock continues its chime—
Tick-tock, tick-tock,
Time is stolen by thieves in
The darkest night, and
Skies feel heavy without the moon.
Predators are lurking,
Bright lights are stolen from the sky—
Until, once again, the moon is reborn
To begin again from its fateful end.

Sparkling Flames

Fire burns flames of life
Flaring crimson red.
Flickering orange phoenixes
Fly high into the seas of longevity.
Crackling light results in ashen wood.
We unite with bonfires,
Ceasing all else, but dancing in celebration.
Calming in depths of darkness, lasting until the final flames.

Amongst all this purity of soul, of energy,
Few flames burn in hues of blues,
Drizzling meek flurries—
Side by side with Sol's children
Are those blinded to light.
Exploded stars, surmounting to nothing.
Death of light—
Hollowed amongst fulfilled.
One by one, blue fires align along cracks,
Escaping fires of the brilliant light, of Sol.

Hundreds feel the quenching heat of the suffocating hellfire,
Ending with halos cresting off Earth's surface.
Down they go, plummeting—
Fleeing from the invisible darkness
To that in plain sight.

Man's Ignorance

It's when one is at the cusp of greatness—
Only then is the fragility that life possesses exposed.
Forevermore, you act maddeningly to ensure ignorance
to trenches.
But it was different before, back when there was nothing to
lose.
Enraptured, captivated by something of a muse—
Your molded, Greek goddess sculpture that could never be
used.
Now, there's doubt—an unquenchable thirst.
You cry rivers of tears and gold, with a crack, and the cup is
ready to spoil its riches.
Fame, glory, power, and wealth—vain along sides of dirty
roads, collecting into ditches.
Basking under the sun no longer.
Gateways to Heaven's doors
crumble—down, fall the divine bridges.
Your success or failure has been finalized within stone.
The muse, the pure creation is now tainted with red—
Your golden compass, you have long discarded,
It now forever sleeps within your enemies' beds.
And like that, no longer is there anything to fend.
You may plead and cry for the cycle to end,
But for another, fresher victim, 'tis soon to begin again.

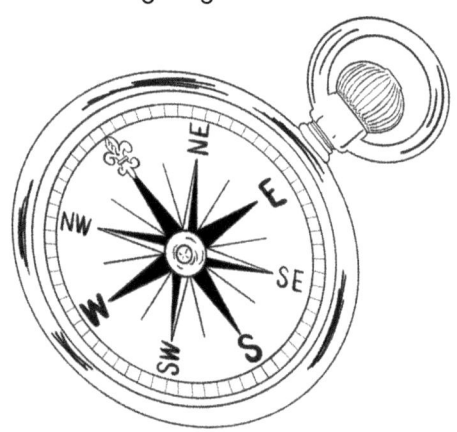

Throne Room

Dedication.
A driven purpose,
Fueling the body, rejuvenating the mind.

Long hours toiling away
Keeping all other prerogatives at bay
Losing sight, sleep idling by.

Paving the path through muck
No end within sight
One breath at a time.

When the time comes,
A king, no longer prince, stands
Among pillars, atop marble.
The succession, that driven desire
Paid off at last.

Fear and envy chill the crowd;
Spiders crawling down spines
Dare everyone to speak a line.

Eyes of viper with golden smiles
Embellishing elegant gowns.
Beads of sweat drip down necks
As ladies and gentlemen dance

To rise to very top
After clawing all the way up,
Left depleted of everything you had—

Bone-cold wine dribbles down upon the throne.
The skies burn red
Leaving hundreds dead.

The floor shudders, leaving everything asunder,
Faded away among rubble and ash.
A bloodied throne abandoned, and
So suddenly
A king forgotten,
A kingdom gone.

Battle

A brawling fight
Eyes of killer mammals,
Mouth threading tracks of saliva.

Potent smells of raw flesh intoxicating
Sweat evaporating,

A heart thirsts for blood—
Pumps, fast, fast, faster—
Blood invigorates the beast,

Pain excites the beast.
Its death will never come.

Watch, as it mocks its prey,
Enslaved to the ring,

Palpitating with fear.
The monster, an enemy, a curse—

Muscles constrict at the body's weakness.
Sight blurred, colored in black and white,
Heart beats slow, slow, slower.

Blood thumps from opened wounds.
Adrenaline stuns to stillness,
Death inevitably comes.

Go, run, donkey—
Flee while you can.

Blindly, the animal charges forward.
Lost in the world of darkness,
Not knowing the paths ahead.

Calmed may the donkey be,
A settling of the mind.
Cleansed from madness and temperament.

Slowly, the monster recedes back into nothing.
Screeching and howling,
Hearing the receded clumps of hooves battering.

It hunches on the lifeless ground below,
Contemplating what should be done next.

Cycling Nature

A mountain dangles high—
Into brisk clouds, it hides.
One step and you fall, and die.
This mountain,
Doomed since its creation

The silent warrior,
Standing for eons amid
changing presents.
Protector, a fighter
Noble guardian.

The great fortress,
Beautiful, daring, formidable
A dead, living thing
that never wavers

But, with time, it withers
Beaten, scorched, trampled
It persists.

Yet, the scars are wedged deeper
And slowly, the old thing lowers.
Sinking further into the earth,
Settling down before a final inhale.

Smoke bellows from its belly,
Miles of sky
Covered under gray.
Quaking, its power
shakes the ground;
Not a creature stirs.
The mountain sinks,
below, into the earth
From which it came.
Left, a mere hole in the ground
And fields of emptiness,
Where a mountain
Once stood.

Remember

Rats roiling above graveyard corpses,
Nails scraping along sandstone,
Uncovering a plague.

A forgotten name,
Living until an unknown year—
Or, had they ever lived?
Resting atop hills,
Or in a slumber within valleys,
Now, never seeming to matter.

Infectious vermin,
Spreading their plague of repugnance
Withering with the brutality of time.

Memory fades, and soon abandoned,
Left, are the unwanted
Keeping the dead company.

Off, the rats travel onward
Trailing pebbles and dirt,
Of graveyard earth.

What Results

Earthquakes leave foundations in shambles
Building up to huge devastations befalling millions.
Houses tumble to the ground,
Lives lost, squashed like bugs.

Aftermath of the blindly raging
Not a thing is left as sweltering indignation is emptied, and
Anger forgotten—
Dissipating as fog lifts.
Ash falls, and
Fight's cease, instantaneously.

Until all that is left is sorrow and regret.
Forever burned in our memories,
Images of a loved one's death.

Spring

Spring begets a journey of new life.
There is a time for everything.
You need to experience life in order to grow from it.
This is your metamorphosis, the journey
you take from child to adult.
Most never feel ready for what's next to come, the
path of change, uncertainty, and unfamiliarity.
But until it's been tried, you will not know.

Childhood

In mere seconds, it passes by, and we are
Thrust into the unknown
Of adulthood.
It's the transition
That makes or breaks you;
That small margin of gray
In which you have to straighten the kinks
Until everything is set in stone.
That number,
That age hangs just above your head—

The party,
The excitement,
The possibilities of adulthood.
The berated questions
Of future,
Of plans,
Of next steps,
The highs and lows.
For better or worse, you're
Not a child anymore.

I'm Going

I'm going where the sun has a destination,
Where apes conquered evil
Where life is light,
And a Paradise bears me fruits of knowledge.
I'm walking forward
In the middle of crossroads.
Endings circling to beginnings
Unforeseen paths to destiny.
I'm from an era of rebirth,
Where the seas have parted.
Walk the path, dig feet on the ocean's floor—
Or succumb to death before all enemies.
Every footfall takes me
To a place,
To a time,
To a future where every breath feels lighter
Where I find my sun, my inner sanctuary.
I'm where I'm supposed to be.

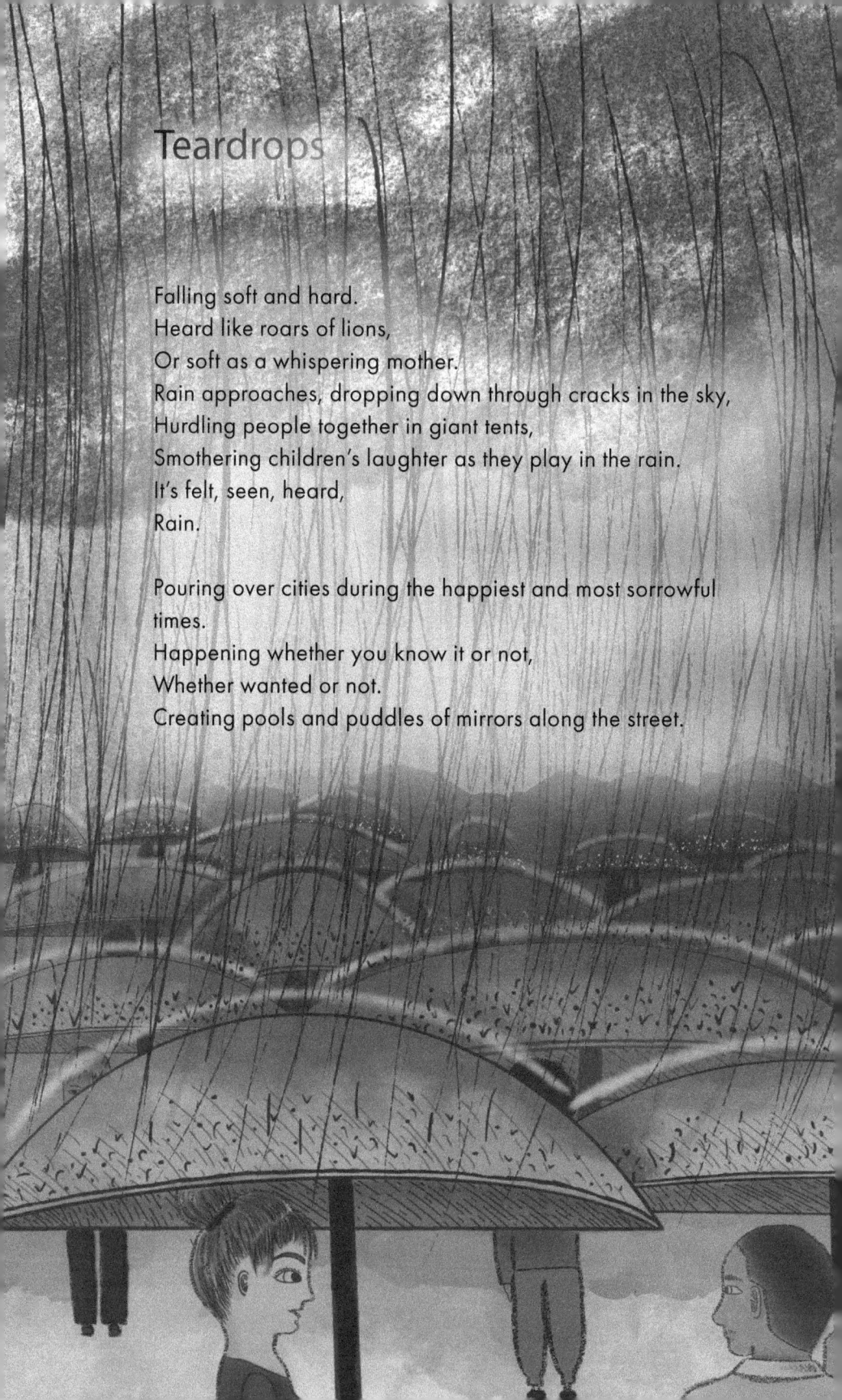

Teardrops

Falling soft and hard.
Heard like roars of lions,
Or soft as a whispering mother.
Rain approaches, dropping down through cracks in the sky,
Hurdling people together in giant tents,
Smothering children's laughter as they play in the rain.
It's felt, seen, heard,
Rain.

Pouring over cities during the happiest and most sorrowful times.
Happening whether you know it or not,
Whether wanted or not.
Creating pools and puddles of mirrors along the street.

Rain
Asks you to pause your day to enjoy sincerity.
It caresses you in your sleep.
Rain is the essence of life,
Sustaining the planet
Pitter patter, pitter patter—
Rain comes knocking on your door.
A smile begins to form
An unwavering excitement for rain.
With greetings of hello or goodbye,
It always gives promise of wondrous things.
Glossy and renewed, the world reappears.
Spreading light
Giving life.

Dream Cloud

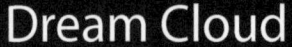

Far beyond, or above
Is where an eye wanders,
Catapulting the mind toward a destination
No impurity could ever touch.
Why must a heart ache
At empty skies?

A child sits on barren earth
Among six- and eight-legged creatures
To imagine a possibility,
While surrounded by aged eyes—
But can only see possibilities of alleged failures.
A collection of dust and water—
Like tumbleweeds—
Migrating with the wind.

Clouds travel the world.
From tundra to desert—
Land to city—
Stretching far across our universe.
Onlooking a sunrise, cresting a mountain shrouded within
morning dew,
Wearily cradled by the sun's setting colors,
Saturating an evening ocean with the colors of embers—
Experiencing day and night
As one.

In the dead of night,
Tufts of cotton march
Leisurely, strolling through skies,
Admiring stars as one›s own canvas.

The camel—
Who lingered for days,
Traveling through grueling desert—
Looks up to the skies and sees
A bird gliding wind currents
Up and down.
A human, born on its back,
Soon dies on its back.
Has always traveled
With a head of stars.

Eons, centuries, decades,
Are stolen by the hands of time.
Clouds will still fly,
Night and day.

Growing Older

It has been coming closer since you were young.
Peering around the corner to experience a first crush,
Witnessing friends who came, and went.
Awaiting adulthood to be delivered by the mailman.
Anxious with worry of any
unforeseen delays.

Elementary thankfully passes and a
big celebration is held.
Age 10, double digits!
No longer are you just some little kid.
You are accomplishing something
grand—
But you aren't an adult yet.

Middle school comes,
Petty hormones arise
And rebellion brews in the bellies of
Angsty preteens—then it's all over.
In the blink of an eye,
The principal is shipping you to high school.
Another farewell, to yet again begin anew.

Hurdled into high school
Pack on your back
As they prepare you for adulthood—

College.
In the end, not much is remembered
But a faint sense of reminiscence while
Waving to classmates and teachers
One last time.

Friends who once circled us
Have long since parted at the fork in the road,
Each on their own journey,
To each their own belonging.

Peering over the shoulder,
There's no escaping it now.
A package arrived at the
doorstep.
It's time to grow up.

Waves of Emotion

In two instances
All falls apart.
One, crumbling under happiness,
Then two, breaking from torments of sadness.

Instances
In just under a second,
Vast expanses of
emotions are
beckoned,
Frail and sore, dreary
hearts are weakened.

Instances
Like an addict, depression hits hard.
Air is churned into an
aura of despair,
Like evil souls
silently screaming, actions futile when
barred.

It's only within
clarity we begin to find
healing,
After great floods of emotions
recede.
The heart is left raw, and eyes
glisten with uncertainty

In between. The purest time in life.

Duality

That indecisive feeling
Body distraught
Brain clouded within a murky mist
With a smile, endless.

Living and dying by each breath,
The torment of a tsunami's wrath
Settles as a rainbow floods the sky.

Dark moments painting a canvas
Light and beautiful treasures refining their art
Suddenly, something is created
Entirely its own.

Importance comes from meaning.
No meaning comes from nothing,
As no one could ever be fulfilled
With just one feeling.

Life is an opportunity.
People, treasures long misused.
Time, a gift no one can repair.

After obstacles are defeated,
Only a smile is left
For a resilience that endures,
And the heart that remains
Dually good and bad
But wise in decision,
And thoughtful of empathy,
With the strength to believe
In both the good,
The bad,
And all in between.

Beyond Dreams

Gaze within your own telescope,
Uncover galaxies only visible to your eye.
Much to explore,
Under moonlight's gaze—
Dried milk drizzled on the horizon,
Promises, wishes, devotions,
Under fluorescent skies.
It only ever expands
Across infinite measures,
Their secrets unbeknownst to all.
The possibilities of their knowledge
May seem tantalizing,
Understanding of the universe—
Everything.
But, can even the stars
contain your dreams?

Pursuing Life

What could life's great meaning be
When we all desire something different?
Must we all fall to the same path
As colonies of ants?
Or
Can we fly as wind
To the extent of our dreams?

All Beginning

In another atmosphere, things would be steady,
Water would have no movement,
Just as leaves would never fall.

Trees would cry in agony as they slowly wither,
Their babies never gazing upon the radiant sun.

Yet, with the smallest droplet,
Water is rippled—
Moving
With grace,
Vigor,
Power,
And the dominoes fall.

Rain.
That which grieves the fallen life
To give rebirth
As it settles back into the replenishing earth,
Which gave it life.
And slowly, new buds bloom
For the sake of all living things.

Life isn't possible without death,
Just as saplings
Never grow in a day.
We are evolving creatures,
Destined to change as the seasons.
Imperfections of man and nature supersede
The mirage of stagnant perfection.
Value that of the
Sun,
Earth,
And moon,
Igniting our stars.
Encircling our world.

We find our sun that enlightens,
We find the moon that balances,
We light our stars, guiding the journey.
And it all begins with that single drop
Of rain,
Paving the way for all our small little worlds,
Patiently waiting
For the next sun.

Life's Definition

Twigs simmer in the wind,
Rattling harmoniously to the orchestra of the forest
Hiding the secrets of life.

The equation of giving and taking,
The chirping of birds and cries of fallen trees
Feel the flight of survival burned into their DNA.

Life is stagnant as a tree,
Reaching toward the sky until its limit.
Life is short as a bug
Life flows like a river,
Everything in its place,
Continuously making the harmonies of life.

In

An array of voices charge,
So clean and crisp;
prim and proper.
"Follow our lead,
Walk down this beaten path."

But there, standing,
There, not marching—
You.

Who are you?
What do you stand on?
Whom do you love?
What are you?

A little nobody—
A confused, indecisive nobody—
A young adolescent nobody.

This person, walking
one step at a time,
Uncovering who they
are bit by bit,

Between

Discovering zest for life,
Exploring the smallest, most
outlandish possibilities,
Adventuring the depths
of their hearts,
Embracing their love
when returning home.
You.

One who experiences the
in-between is no criminal.
Undecided beings are no more
idiotic than the decided.
Confused by who they
are, what they need,
What they desire.

But of one thing they—
you—are sure:
You wish not to be sequestered.

Soar and travel
Through realms of
The Between.

Acknowledgements

    This has been a long and challenging road that wouldn't have been possible without all the encouragement and guiding hands of those around me. Life isn't just about one or two people, it's everyone that has inspired you, set you back, raised you up, and have learned from.
    To my dear teachers, you know who you are, thank you for being there. Pushing me to be the best writer I can, listening to me with sincerity, you guys were always more than teachers to me. Thank you. To my friends of every past, I owe a lot to you. There were definitely hard times, and although we parted ways, it's all thanks to the relationships we formed that molded me into who I am, teaching me a lot about myself, people, and learning how to become someone better. For all the good and bad, I give my gratitude and wish you the best luck in your futures.
    To the family members that I no longer have communications with, it was you guys who made, what I think, are the biggest lessons and challenges for me to learn and overcome. Thank you for every experience. And to my treasured family, I owe a lot to you, thank you and I love you.
    Most importantly, I give my appreciation to all of my readers. I am humbled by you, and are the reason why I write. Building something greater than yourself, pushing past any fear and obstacle to create something remarkable. It may have striken you, maybe it didn't resonate with you. Thats okay, thank you for giving me a chance. To those who understood, who had poems speaking to your life, I published these poems to let you know you aren't alone. Something I so desired when I was younger.
    Take from it what you will, and discard the rest.

Author Bio

Penny Sage started writing at an early age as a way to express her voice and reflect on the world around her. She loves her cat, sweets, and helping build up those around her.

www.ingramcontent.com/pod-product-compliance
Lightning Source LLC
LaVergne TN
LVHW051039070526
838201LV00066B/4861